Mystery at the Bike Race

Mystery at the Bike Race

BY FRANK TOPPER

Illustrations by Jackie Rogers

TROLL ASSOCIATES

Library of Congress Cataloging in Publication Data

Topper, Frank.
     Mystery at the bike race.

     (Solve-it-yourself)
     Summary: As you, the reader, work on a newspaper story
about your town's annual bicycle race, your suspicions
are aroused that something sinister is happening involving
the new electronics plant.
          1. Plot-your-own stories.   2. Children's stories,
American.   [1. Mystery and detective stories.   2. Plot-
your-own stories]   I. Rogers, Jackie, ill.   II. Title.
III. Series.
PZ7.T6443My   1985   [Fic]   84-16452
ISBN 0-8167-0454-6 (lib. bdg.)
ISBN 0-8167-0455-4 (pbk.)

10   9   8   7   6   5   4   3   2   1

Warning!

In this story, *you* are the detective! *You* must find the clues, follow the leads, and try to solve the mystery.

But do not read this book from beginning to end. Start on page 1, and keep reading till you come to a choice. After that, the story is up to you. Your decisions will take you from page to page.

Think carefully before you decide. Some choices will lead you to further clues. But other choices may bring about a quick end to your investigation—and to you!

Whatever happens, you can always go back to the beginning and start again. Best of luck in your investigation.

Every summer for the last twenty-five years, the Great Watertown Bicycle Race has been the highlight of the year in your town. In the early days of the race, the competitors were a small group of local cyclists. Five years ago, the Clean and Sweet Soap Company started sponsoring the race.

By signing a network-television agreement, the soap company was able to attract nationwide attention for tomorrow's race. Now, many outstanding riders from all over the world compete in the race. This year's race has the largest number of contestants ever—more than 175 top cyclists.

The racecourse ranges over eighty-three miles of hilly roads, starting in distant Cedarville and ending in Watertown. Much of the road runs along the Willow River, which was once used to send timber downstream to Watertown. The racers compete for individual and team honors. Each team has six members—three men and three women.

You've competed in several local races, and someday you think you might want to enter the big Watertown race. But this year you are much too busy. You have a job after school working as a reporter for the Watertown *Weekly Dispatch*. Sam Jenkins, the editor and owner of the paper, has personally trained you.

Mr. Jenkins, or "Mr. Sam," was a former Chicago police reporter who moved to Watertown after a successful career of writing about big-city crime.

Mr. Sam has shown you how to track down stories in a professional way, using some of the experience that helped him win national prominence when he worked in Chicago. Mr. Sam suggests that you cover the race on your new motorbike.

"Since you know the route pretty well," he says, "you might find it interesting to report on what the race is really like from the cyclists' point of view. Take my portable tape recorder and a few extra tapes to make notes. I hear a lot of the riders are going down to the Super Gear Cycle and Sport Shop to get some last-minute equipment. Why don't you go down there and talk to some of the riders and their coaches? And you'd better check with the people at the soap company, too."

"Wheels" Wilson is the owner of the Super Gear Cycle and Sport Shop. Although you don't know him that well, you know that Wheels is a former cyclist who hurt himself in a nasty spill going up Snake Hill in the Watertown race seven years ago.

Wheels' store has established itself as the gathering place for local cyclists all year round. Talk in the store often ends up with how Wheels could have

won the Watertown race that year if it hadn't been for "that darn hill." Today the store is crowded with cyclists and bike fans.

Wheels knows you from the local races you've competed in. As you walk into the shop, he asks, "Are you riding in the race tomorrow?"

"I'd like to," you say. "But I want to write a story on the race for the *Dispatch*.

When Wheels hears this, he tells you again about his Snake Hill experience. "You know, that's the best place to watch the race," he says. "Right at the top of the hill, next to that new electronics plant."

As you walk out of the store, you are attracted by one of the bike-support vehicles—the vans that carry the spare bikes and supplies in major races. The van you notice is dark gray with silver lettering. Since you can't make out what it says from where you are, you move closer. The silver letters spell out SLICK MESSENGER SERVICE.

You've heard of the Slick Messengers' bike-racing team, and you don't know whether to believe what's been said. You've heard several stories about their dirty racing tactics.

As you approach the Slick van, you overhear two men, standing next to it, talking about the race. Suddenly one of them changes the subject.

"The electronics plant is right at the top of Snake Hill," he says. "Are you sure everything's ready?" The other man nods.

The first man slowly bends down to tie one of his shoelaces. That's when you notice the unusual shoes both of the men are wearing. Although they are wearing normal street clothes, their shoes are the kind that top bicycle racers wear. And these shoes are decorated with an unusual red design on each side. Both men stare at you for a moment.

You keep walking down the street, your mind posing several questions at once. These two are up to *something*, but what?

If you decide to call Mr. Sam and tell him what you overheard, turn to page 17.

If you decide to wait until the two men leave the van, and then try to find out what's inside it, turn to page 44.

If you decide to go back inside the cycle shop and tell Wheels what you suspect, turn to page 49.

What's the connection between Joseph and Mr. Murray? There's only one way to find out. You go over to Mr. Murray and ask him if he's interested in the race.

"Yes, I am, from a security standpoint," he says. "As you know, the race goes right by the Contron plant. The TV people wanted to use our front lawn to set up their cameras, but I just couldn't allow it. National security is at stake.

"I also happen to know Joseph for a long time. I'm a real fan of his," continues Mr. Murray. "If you want a good story, I suggest you follow him as closely as you can. He's the best. I helped his parents get settled in this country when I was with the FBI. I'll be watching him myself. I always do."

"What makes Joseph worth watching?" you ask Mr. Murray.

"Joseph has a special talent for measuring the stamina of other riders, waiting until they tire, and then sprinting past them near the finish line," says Mr. Murray. "He's already won three races this year using that strategy. But the Watertown race is going to be his toughest, especially with all the foreign teams."

So that's why the security manager is so interested in Joseph. But that still doesn't explain Mr. Murray's behavior with you earlier today. You decide to push your luck and ask him about your earlier conversation.

"When I was at your plant this morning, I still had a funny feeling that something out of the ordinary was going on," you say.

Mr. Murray apologizes for being so abrupt. "We have to be alert all the time," he explains. "When events like the race are near one of our plants, we add extra security. Recently, one of our plants out west was burglarized when a county fair opened nearby. Unfortunately, all the normal noise and activity of a fair, or a race like this, can create diversions for criminals. We have to be extra careful."

You thank Mr. Murray for all the information. The race goes off the next day. Joseph takes second place, and you write a fine story about the race.

But the next day you hear the terrible news. The Contron plant was somehow robbed during the race. Valuable electronics secrets are missing, and so is Contron's security manager, Kurt Murray. You will always wonder what really happened.

THE END

from page 20

Not quite trusting Mr. Slick, you politely decline his offer and return to the newspaper office. After going over all of your notes, you decide to write a feature story about Joseph and his special bikes. But first you tell Mr. Sam the rumors you've heard about Mr. Slick and his team.

Mr. Sam says, "I've heard those same rumors, but I don't believe them. Bill Slick has one of the best teams in the country. They train hard. I think some of their competitors make up those stories about dirty racing tactics. The Slick people never try to fight the rumors; they just go out and win races.

"Sometimes you get lucky when one story leads to a bigger one. But in this case you don't have much to go on. You'd better stick to a straightforward story about the race."

You finish your story, realizing that you must stick to the facts to do your job. And suspicions are not facts. Nevertheless, you still remain suspicious of the Slick bike-racing team.

After thinking it over, you decide to call Mr. Slick and accept his offer to let you ride in the Slick support van. When you finally reach him at his hotel later in the day, he is out for the night. You leave a message, but he never returns your call.

The next day, you hear that the Slick van met with a mysterious accident during the race and skidded into a ditch. Luckily, no one was hurt.

After the race, you overhear one of the officials talking to the sheriff. "Do you really think that someone connected with the race would deliberately cut the tires on Slick's van just to win?"

"We think it's a possibility," says the sheriff. "You say Slick's the best, and some people will do anything just to win." Later, you spot Mr. Slick at the finish line, talking to the officials and the sheriff. When you mention the accident to Mr. Slick, he tells you that they hit an oil slick. You try questioning the other teams, but no one knows what happened, or how it happened.

You have failed to uncover any evidence of wrongdoing, but you still have a good story on the race.

THE END

You leave the security manager's office and head back to town on your motorbike. How did Mr. Murray know about the bike shoes with the strange design? And does he really have those reports? He didn't actually show them to you. He waved some papers around and showed you pictures of the two men. But you didn't get a look at any "reports."

At a fast-food restaurant, you find a pay phone and call Mr. Sam. He agrees that something is up at the plant. "You'd better get back to town and try finding those two fellows at the bike store," says Mr. Sam. "Turn on the recorder when you talk to them. And be careful."

Back in town, as you near the bike shop, you spot the two men. They are still hanging around in front of the Slick Messenger van. You walk over to the men and explain to them that you're covering the race for the *Dispatch*. You ask them for an interview, and they both agree to talk to you. In fact, they are quite pleasant.

You find out that the younger of the two men has been a racer for Slick for five years. Because he was such a fast bike messenger, the owners of the business made him a member of their racing team. His name is Joseph. He was born in Russia and came to this country when he was five years old.

"In our last race, we jumped out in front of the pack early and stayed there for the entire race," says Joseph. "No one caught up to us. Would you like to see one of our custom-made bikes? If you're careful, I'll let you ride my backup bike."

You find out that Joseph can speak three foreign languages—French, German, and Russian. His father got him interested in bike racing and helped him build his first competitive bike.

You look at Joseph's bike in amazement. He tells you that the parts come from all over the world: a shiny red frame from England, brakes from Italy, gears from Japan, and pedals from France.

If Joseph is as good as his bike, you think to yourself, he's probably the one to watch in this race. You might be talking to the winner-to-be.

Kurt Murray, the security manager at Contron, is also in town. He must have driven in when you left his office. Mr. Murray is talking to one of the TV commentators who have come to Watertown to cover the race.

Then you notice something interesting. As Joseph bends down to show you his special silk racing tires, you catch him smiling at Mr. Murray.

If you want to find out if there is a connection between Joseph and Mr. Murray, turn to page 7.

If you think Joseph was just being friendly, and if you would like to accept his invitation to ride one of his bikes, turn to page 19.

14

You decide to check the motels. But first you go back to the paper and tell Mr. Sam what you learned at the library. He thinks that you might have an important story about the electronics burglaries.

You go through the phone book and find the addresses of the four motels. They are all near one another on the main road near the electronics plant. You call each motel and learn that one of them does have a Slick Messenger Service van in its parking lot.

You ride out to the Watertown Chalet, the motel where the van was spotted. The owner of the motel is Fred Ross, a retired army colonel. He tells you that he registered two men in Room 305. The registration card says that both men, Tom Willis and Peter Furth, work for Wolverine Data Products in Chicago. You wait in the front lobby until both men come out of their room. You are certain they are the same men you saw earlier in the day.

If these men really work for a computer company, they could be connected to a possible robbery of electronic devices. You slip into a phone booth and report this to Agent Hooper at his office. He tells you to stay away from the men and their room until he gets to the motel.

Agent Hooper gets to the motel office in five minutes. Just as he enters the office, the two men walk out to the van. They open the rear doors and start taking electronic equipment back to their room. Mr. Hooper calls his office to get backup help. In a few minutes, two local police officers show up at the motel. Mr. Hooper tells them where to place themselves when he knocks on the motel-room door. He draws his gun and enters the room. After a few minutes, he comes out of the motel room, smiling.

"Apparently, these fellows are here to help computerize the standings of tomorrow's race for future use by the national team," he says. "All the races and performances for the entire year will be put into the computer to help select and train the team. They borrowed the Slick Messenger Service van to get around. It won't be needed by the Slick team until tomorrow."

Later in the day, the two men invite you into their room to show you the way the computer predicts how most of the riders will perform.

Oh, well, you didn't uncover any wrongdoing, but you did solve a mystery. And you'll be able to write an up-to-the-minute story on computers and bike racing.

THE END

You call Mr. Sam and tell him your suspicions. "There were two men hanging around near the Slick Messenger Service van," you say. "They said something about the new electronics plant."

"Come back to the office right away," Mr. Sam says. "This could be important. We'll try to check it out."

When you get back to the newspaper office, Mr. Sam shows you how to research a story by using the *Dispatch*'s "morgue," a huge file that contains a copy of every back issue of the paper. You find out that the first Cedarville-to-Watertown bicycle race was more like a parade than a race. Each succeeding year, though, the racers took the challenge more seriously.

As you go through the old papers in the file, you find out that Wheels Wilson was once one of the top cyclists in the country. But seven years ago, after losing the Watertown race, he suddenly dropped out of sight. For two years no one in town knew what had happened to him. Five years ago Wheels returned to Watertown and opened his bike shop. Where had he been for those two years? There was nothing in the files.

You now turn your attention to the electronics plant. All you can find in the back issues is an article that appeared in the *Dispatch* three summers ago. The article announced that a new electronics plant would be constructed in Cedarville. Contron, Inc., a division of Allworth Industries, was building the plant. Most of the work at the plant would be done under government contract.

Contron, the article said, was headed by Cedric Wheyworth, a brilliant executive about whom little was known at the time. The follow-up stories in later issues of the *Dispatch* did not give the nature of Contron's or Allworth Industries' business. All you are able to find out is that Contron and Allworth are defense contractors for the government.

This isn't much to go on. What made those men talk about the electronics plant?

If you decide to go to the public library to find out more about Contron, Allworth Industries, and Cedric Wheyworth, turn to page 122.

If you decide to go back to Wheels' shop to get more information about the race from the cyclists and officials, turn to page 121.

You decide to accept Joseph's invitation, which offers you the chance to get some firsthand information for your race story. He helps you get up onto his backup bike. Since you are about the same size as Joseph, the bike fits you pretty well.

"How long did it take you to build a bike like this?" you ask.

"Once we decided on the parts," Joseph says, "it took us only about a month to get them all and put the bike together. After that we added some extras that made it ride even better."

When you go for a spin down the street on Joseph's bike, you notice how smoothly the gears shift and how easy the bike is to maneuver. When you come back from the ride, you see Wheels Wilson, the bike-shop owner, talking to Joseph and an older man. The man looks like Joseph's team manager.

"That's some bike you have, Joseph," says Wheels as you approach. "If this is your backup, what's your number-one bike like?"

"It's practically the same," he says, "only some of the parts are newer."

Wheels introduces you to Mr. William Slick, the president of Slick Messenger Service and manager of their bike-racing team. When Mr. Slick hears that you are covering the race for the *Dispatch*, he asks if you would like to ride in his team's support van during the race.

"You can learn how we help our team," Mr. Slick says. "And perhaps you'll find out that the Slick team is a very good one—maybe the best. I think you'll get a real education in the sport of bicycle racing. All you have to do is watch the race and stay out of the way of the people in the van."

If you want to accept the invitation to ride in the support van, turn to page 25.

If you think Mr. Slick is trying to get you out of the way, turn to page 9.

from page 122

Miss Swanson tells you that she has plenty of information on the history of the Watertown race. She also gives you several books on bike racing.

You learn that most of the winners of previous Cedarville-to-Watertown bicycle races have been foreigners. The only local racer with the skill, stamina, and talent that might have made him a winner was Wheels Wilson.

Wheels had won several big races in his career. But in his last race before he retired, the Watertown race, he crashed mysteriously. No one could figure out what happened. One article reported, "It seemed as though an alien force threw him to the ground and held him back." An old photo of Wheels shows him in a Slick team jersey.

You look further in the newspaper files and find more pictures of Wheels and the Slick racing team. Wheels, you discover, was one of the first members of the Slick team.

The team was formed by a Mr. William Slick to help young people who had been in trouble and needed to accomplish something worthwhile. Most of them were given jobs with his bicycle-messenger service. The best riders became team members. In one article, the writer quotes Mr. Slick: "Most of these young people just need a chance to show that they can do an honest day's work and stay out of trouble. When I got in trouble as a youngster, it was pretty rough for me to get a fresh start."

You also find an article about Wheels. The story is headlined "Wheels Wilson Sentenced to Two Years in Jail for Burglary." The story was written ten years ago.

You decide to copy the articles that you will need as background for your story on the race. When you are at the copying machine, you see a man in a dark sport coat talking to Miss Swanson. She points at you, and the man walks toward you.

"I'm Martin Hooper," he tells you, as he presents his ID and an FBI badge. He lets you finish copying, then escorts you to the library office.

"Why are you making all these inquiries into Contron Electronics?" Mr. Hooper asks.

You tell him about the two suspicious men and how you heard them mention the electronics plant. As a reporter covering the race, you thought you might have a real scoop on possible foul play during the race. You give Mr. Hooper a description of the men, and he asks you to go with him to where you last saw the men and the van.

When you arrive at the spot, the van is no longer there. The FBI agent asks you to go with him to the sheriff's office, where the two of you go over pictures of various wanted criminals. When you look them over, you think you recognize one of the two men that you noticed next to the Slick van.

Agent Hooper asks you if anyone else has seen these men. You tell Hooper, "Wheels Wilson knows them, I think. I saw him wave to them from inside the store." Then you show him your copy of the article on Wheels' jail sentence. "I know all about Wheels," Hooper tells you.

When you return to the shop with Agent Hooper, he questions Wheels. Wheels remembers the two men that he saw in the van in front of the shop. "I never saw them before today," he tells Hooper. "They said they weren't contestants, just bike-racing fans."

You are still suspicious. As you and Agent Hooper leave the store, you tell him that you are sure those men are up to no good.

"I'm glad you're keeping your eyes open," says Hooper. "I'm also glad to have your help." He tells you that he is on a special assignment to prevent thefts from local electronics plants. It seems that shipments of micro-chips valued at millions of dollars have been stolen from the two plants in this area. He wants you to help him find those two men in the van.

If you decide to help Agent Hooper and go back to Wheels' shop on your own, to find out more about the men, turn to page 114.

If you think the men may still be in the area, and decide to check the four motels in Watertown, turn to page 14.

from page 20

You don't want to pass up the invitation to ride in the van. Early the next morning, the day of the race, you meet Mr. Slick, Joseph, and five other team members to go to the starting line in Cedarville. When you get into the van, you notice labeled compartments of all sizes, full of assorted bicycle parts. Mr. Slick points out all the different items that they carry for the team. Then you notice a large two-way radio.

"What do you use the radio for?" you ask.

"To keep in touch with our other van," says Mr. Slick. "We also use it in case of accidents, to call the police or an ambulance."

When the van gets to Cedarville, you sense the excitement. The television cameras seem to be everywhere. A TV commentator interviews Joseph at the starting line.

As you scan the assembled racers, you see another member of the Slick team talking to one of the men you saw near the van in Watertown yesterday. The Slick team member looks frightened.

The starter's gun goes off. In a matter of seconds, 175 racing bikes go flying down the road. You can see Joseph in his black, red, and silver jersey at the front of the pack. The frightened team member you saw earlier is just ahead of Joseph. You ask who he is.

"That's Carl," says Mr. Slick. "He's going to start breaking the wind so Joseph can draft. When you draft, you ride behind someone, taking advantage of that person's breaking the air ahead of you. Riding with less wind resistance can save ten to fifteen percent of your energy."

Carl clearly has the lead, and Joseph is right behind him. Everyone in the van is straining to look out the windows, trying to see how far ahead of the pack their riders are.

After the first twenty miles, there are two groups of riders—the main body and the breakaway group, where Joseph and Carl are in the lead. As the race hits the halfway mark, the riders maintain their positions. They are conserving their energy for the tough climb up Snake Hill.

"Let's make sure the people in the other van at the bottom of Snake Hill know we're coming their way. Get on the radio!" commands Mr. Slick. The message goes out, but the other van doesn't answer.

Mr. Slick looks puzzled. "Where are they?" he asks. "Something must be wrong."

One of the other support-team members in the van tells Mr. Slick, "It's probably just bad reception. There might be interference from the electronics equipment at the plant."

If you agree that it is bad radio reception, turn to page 35.

If you think something else is wrong, turn to page 110.

You go left at the fork and run into a series of hills. You quickly shift gears for the first hill. After riding for a couple of minutes, you realize that there are no other racers in sight. You must have taken the wrong turn at the fork.

Just then, you remember the radio in your helmet. You turn it on and get a great deal of static.

"Slick Two, this is Mobile One. Do you read me?" you say again and again.

Finally you hear the voice of Mr. Durdeen. He is asking for your position. You tell him where you are. He tells you to go up the road for another half mile. You'll come to an intersection.

"Go right at the crossroads," he says, "and you'll be back on course."

You tell him about being pushed. He says that the crash might have been caused intentionally by a member of the Red Beetle gang. When you hear the "Red Beetle" name, you remember reading about them. They are a gang of international terrorists and thieves who work for anyone who is willing to pay their price. Hearing their name makes you nervous.

"The Red Beetles are the ones we're after, and it seems they always disappear before we can identify them. I would have warned you, but I didn't want to alarm you before the race."

Mr. Durdeen tells you to be careful when you catch up to the pack.

You follow his directions, and in a matter of minutes you again approach the main body of racing cyclists.

You realize that this is not the right way to ride a race. You would normally be disqualified if you took a shortcut, but this is special: You're working for the FBI!

You feel stronger now, but just as you really start to move, your front tire hisses. More bad luck! You have a flat.

Suddenly the rider in front of you turns around and smiles at you. "Tough luck. Too tacky for you," he says. You can't see his face clearly, because he's riding into the sun and wearing sunglasses. But you do see the tacks he dropped. Two of them are stuck in your tire. Luckily, you get a glimpse of the number on the man's racing jersey.

Soon your support van comes up and helps you change the tire. But by the time you are set to ride again, the main body of cyclists is once more far ahead of you.

You ride off in pursuit. Although you don't catch up to the cyclists, you do finish the race and receive a small prize for being the youngest finisher.

But the best reward of all comes from Mr. Durdeen several weeks later. You get a letter from him and the FBI, thanking you for the information you gave them that led to the capture and arrest of the Red Beetle gang.

You are glad to be of help. And you have to admit you had a good time being a competitive cyclist. In fact, you can't wait to enter next year's Great Watertown Race on your own.

THE END

30

The two men walk over to a big red van with blue trim. A sign on the side of the van says Fire Flyers. The emblem underneath the legend is a bike wheel with fiery wings.

"I thought you were members of the Slick team," you say.

"No," says one, "we were just standing and talking near the Slick van when you came around."

"We're Watertown firefighters," says the other. "That's why we have the 'Fire Flyers' emblem on our van and on our equipment."

As interesting as this information is, you wonder why they are so eager to talk to you. They open up their van and show you a new twelve-speed bike.

"It's the hottest bike on the circuit," another proud firefighter says from inside the van. "Pick it up."

The bike is so light that you can pick it up with only two fingers. One of the Fire Flyers tells you that the bike weighs only eighteen pounds. It was made from a special alloy, titanium, that is used in the manufacture of spacecraft and rockets.

There may be a story here, but there's nothing mysterious about the Fire Flyers. You decide to check out the Slick van.

Turn to page 44.

You just don't trust these men, and you politely decline their invitation. You decide to go back to the newspaper office to talk to Mr. Sam.

On your way back to the office, you meet Sheriff Stryker and tell him about the two men you saw hanging around the bike shop. Your suspicions prove to be correct. Sheriff Stryker reads you a description of the two men from a piece of paper.

"They're big-time bicycle thieves, wanted in several states," he tells you. "They hang around bike races posing as riders. Then they hop on one of the bikes and ride it into a rented van or truck parked nearby. We're lucky you had your eyes open. I've been looking for them, but I haven't seen them around."

The sheriff hurries over to his patrol car and radios for help. In less than two minutes, his officers track down the thieves. They were about to steal two very valuable bikes.

You call in your story to the *Dispatch* office. "With a little more experience," says Mr. Sam, "you'll be a fine big-city crime reporter. I'm proud of you."

That night Ed Leffel of the soap company calls and thanks you for helping keep the race free of crime. He offers you a ride in the official helicopter to watch the race. You will be able to see every mile.

Your story for the paper turns out to be the best coverage of the bike race that the *Dispatch* ever had.

THE END

from page 46

It's just too risky to make a break for it. Deciding to take your chances hidden in the van, you listen to the two men arguing as they stand outside the rear door. Suddenly the door swings open. The men continue to argue. But just as quickly as it opened, the door swings shut again.

"I don't care what he says. We can't get past the Contron fence without Security seeing us."

"All right," says the other man. "Let's have another look at the plans. Open the van."

You hide under the steering wheel. The van smells oily and stuffy. It is hard not to sneeze. The men grope around in the dark for the flashlight.

"I've got it," one of them says.

"Bring it here," says the other, "so I can get it on the plan book."

You figure the plan book must be the book you were looking at. But what are they using it for? They start flipping through the pages.

"Charlie, this laser decoder is fantastic. It looks just like a regular flashlight."

They stop at one page and read it over slowly.

You can see their barely reflected faces in the window. The one called Charlie looks older, and seems to be in charge. "Scoot," Charlie says to the other man, "we'd better check with the boss about this. This is one tough job, and I don't want to foul it up. Let's go."

"All right," the other man says. "But we better radio Mr. B. that we're coming over."

"Okay. Turn on the radio and give him the signal," Charlie says.

"Mr. B., this is the Scooter. *The lights are dim and our battery needs charging.*"

A voice through the receiver speaker replies, "Roger. Take it to the old garage on the main highway outside of town."

"We read you, Mr. B. Roger and out."

The men put back the book and the laser decoder. They leave the van, and you watch them drive away in another car. You slip out of the van a few minutes later.

The street is empty, and you breathe a sigh of relief. You don't know what you would have done if they had found you.

Now that you're safe, your thoughts turn again to the deepening mystery. Who is Mr. B.? And what are his men up to?

You know you're onto a big story, but now you have to make the right move.

If you decide to call Watertown's Sheriff Stryker, turn to page 42.

If you would rather talk to Mr. Sam, turn to page 89.

You were right. It was bad reception. Someone had accidentally turned down the aerial. When you point this out to Mr. Slick, he thanks you and adjusts the antenna properly.

"Hello, Slick One. This is Slick Two. Do you read me?" crackles a voice over the radio.

"That's Harry in our Number Two van," Mr. Slick says, turning to you. "What's going on, Harry? We've been trying to get you."

"I think we have some trouble on the road," Harry says. "There's a huge pile-up halfway down the hill. Someone's thrown rocks on the road, and nobody got through. Hey, wait a minute! Are you near the plant?"

Mr. Slick tells Harry that he can see the electronics plant quite clearly. It's only about a thousand yards away. There is some strange blue smoke coming out of the main entrance, and several security guards are lying on the ground, unconscious. Mr. Slick gets on the radio to call the police.

When your van pulls up to the main gate, you spot two men with gas masks running out of the plant. They are both carrying guns and briefcases. Because of all the noise and confusion, they don't seem to have spotted your van yet. As soon as they get out of the range of the dense blue smoke, the two men throw

away their gas masks. They seem to be running straight toward your van, but you can see what they are actually running toward. An unattended van is parked in front of you on the side of the road. That must be the van the criminals used to get here.

Against Mr. Slick's better judgment, you persuade him to drive you over to the getaway van. You get out of your van and climb into the getaway van's front seat. As you had guessed, there is no one inside. The Slick van moves down the road and waits. If only you can drive this van, the criminals will not be able to get away. But the key is gone! The crooks haven't seen you yet, but they're almost upon you.

You have one last hope, and you find what you're looking for: a gas canister. The two men must have used canisters like this one to overpower the plant's security guards. The canisters seem simple to use: Just pull a small pin and the gas is released.

You hop out of the other side of the van, away from the two men, and climb under the rear of the van. You don't have to wait long. The two men climb into their van and start the engine. They are about to make their escape.

You pull the pin on the canister, open the rear door of the van, throw the smoking canister inside, and slam the door. Everything happens very quickly after that.

Mr. Murray, Contron's security manager, pulls out of the plant's parking lot in his own car and speeds after the smoke-filled van. But the van doesn't get far. The two choking criminals surrender to him without a fight, and the police arrive a few minutes later.

"Wow. It all happened so fast," you say.

"That's what they wanted," says Mr. Murray. "But they didn't count on your quick thinking. Well, it looks like you got your story," he adds, with a wink. "But I'll bet a lot of newspapers will now want to get a story about *you*." He leads you into a side office of the plant and introduces you to his boss, Mr. Cedric Wheyworth.

"Those two men were foreign agents, trying to steal the plans for our latest anti-missile screening system," Mr. Wheyworth says, after thanking you. "This project is so secret that most of the people in the plant don't even know what they're working on."

Mr. Wheyworth goes on to tell you that the security guards at Contron knew that something might happen during the race, but they didn't know how the agents were going to try it. "So we just stayed inside the security office and watched the agents on the closed-circuit TV monitor.

"Thanks to my good friend Bill Slick," Wheyworth continues, "we were able to have his racers create a diversion to give us the help we needed. Slick's team went past the plant just a little faster than anyone ever expected. His racers' quick approach to the plant threw the agents' timing off. Three of the Slick riders got through before the rocks landed on the road. But even then the agents gave us trouble. Thanks to you, they're now behind bars."

Mr. Wheyworth is, in reality, a wonderful person. You have a fascinating conversation with him. Mr. Slick works for him, you learn—Slick Messenger Service is owned by Allworth Industries. Later, you head back to the newspaper office to write your story, and to answer questions from the big-city reporters. You miss the finish of the race, but you find out later that Joseph won. The Slick team also won the team trophy.

You've got more than one scoop in your coverage of the bike race. And you're one of the few people in the last twenty years to have met the mysterious Cedric Wheyworth. Altogether, you've had a pretty good day.

THE END

from page 95

You return to the newspaper office and tell Mr. Sam what the nurse at the plant said. He agrees with you that something may be going on.

"But until we get some hard facts," he says, "I want you to cover the race and do a thorough job of it. In the meantime, I'll call a few of my contacts and see if they can come up with more information about the van."

Mr. Sam hands you several articles about the sport of bike racing and some stories on last year's race. After two hours of wading through background material, you come across a photo of the two men you saw earlier today. The men are too far from the camera, but you can easily identify the mystery van in the photo. You run into Mr. Sam's office to show him your discovery. He looks at the picture and then takes a magnifying glass from his desk drawer to look more closely. He hands you the magnifying glass and asks, "Are you sure those are the men you saw?"

You stare at the picture for a long time. "I'm almost certain," you say.

"I think you'd better go back to race headquarters," says Mr. Sam. "Maybe one of the officials can identify them."

When you get to race headquarters, you show the picture to several officials. No one can identify the men. But one of the riders tells you that the two men in the photo are from the selection committee that picks the national team—the team that will represent our country in the next Olympic Games.

"Since this race is one of the last of the season," he tells you, "it's important that they check out the course, to see if it meets the standards for selecting the team." The rider points out the two men you are trying to find. Both are sitting behind a table going over details of the race with other officials.

After watching them for several minutes, you introduce yourself to them. They both laugh when you tell them about your suspicions. One of them says, "We plan to wait at the top of Snake Hill to see who the best hill climbers are."

They show you computer reports on the riders who will probably be on the next Olympic team. You get all the information you need, then go back to the paper to write a story on the importance of this year's race.

THE END

42

You run over to the sheriff's office to tell him what you've heard and seen. You can see that he's busy with some bike-race officials. After waiting for about ten minutes, you go in to see Sheriff Stryker.

You tell the sheriff about the van. He asks you to repeat your story slowly.

"Well," the sheriff says, "it sounds as if we should take a look at this mysterious van."

When you get to the van, the doors are locked. The sheriff looks a little puzzled.

"You said that you left a door open," he says. "Someone must have come back and locked it."

Two men approach from the rear. One of them asks the sheriff, "Can we help you?"

You recognize the men as Charlie and Scoot, the men you saw in the van.

"Say, fellows," the sheriff says, "I'd like to look inside your van. Don't mind, do you?"

"Go right ahead," Charlie says.

Charlie opens the rear door and turns on a bright overhead lamp. Sheriff Stryker uses his hand-held radio to call for a backup patrol car. He looks through all the drawers and in the radio box. He finds nothing unusual —no laser flashlight, no secret-code book, just bike parts. Did you misread the situation?

He asks the men about the radio. They say they use it during races to keep in touch with their other van and, in emergencies, to call the police.

The sheriff thanks them, and they close and lock the van. "I think you've taken me on a wild-goose chase," he says to you.

Just then a dark sedan pulls up, carrying three men in suits. They nod at the sheriff, and he walks over to the car. The four of them talk.

After they talk, Sheriff Stryker walks back to you and says, "It seems that you've stumbled onto a secret government operation. Those men in the car are from the FBI. They want to talk with you."

You get into the back of the car. "The van you saw is a government surveillance van," one of the men tells you, "posing as a race-support vehicle. The men inside the van are on our staff.

"We're investigating an international gang of thieves who specialize in stealing highly technical electronics gear and selling it to unfriendly nations. To keep an eye on them, we put together a special team of agents who could race bicycles. Their job is to watch out for any suspicious people in or around the race. Unfortunately, they've all mysteriously come down with food poisoning.

"Would you be willing to race for our team tomorrow?" he asks. "We could really use your help. But I have to warn you—it might be dangerous."

If you accept the offer to ride in the race, turn to page 58.

If you are still suspicious about what you saw and heard in the van, turn to page 47.

44

from page 6 / from page 30

You walk to the nearby race headquarters. There you patiently wait outside, around the corner from where the Slick team's van is parked. After it gets dark you'll have a better chance of investigating without being seen.

An hour after sunset, you hear the doors of the van being slammed shut, then voices fading away. Peering around the corner, you spot the same two men walking toward a nearby diner. You cautiously walk up to the van and casually look in the window as you pass by. It's too difficult to see anything inside.

Should you stop and get a closer look? The street is now deserted.

Placing your hand on the van's rear-door handle, you turn it slowly. You carefully check the street again, glancing in all directions. With a quick step, you hop inside the van and shut the rear door tightly. Your heart is pounding.

As you crawl toward the front of the van, you stumble on a flashlight on the bare metal floor. Grateful for the help it will give you, you carefully shine the light around the inside of the van. There isn't much to see. Just lots of parts for bikes and some bike frames. Most of the frames have foreign names on them.

You notice a big gray box on the floor of the van, behind the front passenger's seat. You open a door on the side of the box and discover a large radio. It looks like a CB radio, but if that's what it is, it's the biggest one you've ever seen. Beside the radio is what appears to be a bike-racing rule book.

When you open up the book, you discover that it's written in a foreign language, one whose alphabet you can't even recognize. You turn the book sideways to get a better look at one of the illustrations. As the beam of the flashlight hits the page, the print seems to change. All of a sudden, sentences start to appear in English. Wow! You flip back to the beginning of the book and shine the flashlight on the first page. At the top, the first sentence reads "Contron AMIGS Project—Priority One." You figure that the light somehow activates the type. When you turn the flashlight away, the letters go back to their original appearance.

Just then, before you can read more, you hear voices approaching the van. They sound similar to the voices of the two men you heard earlier in the day. Quickly, you crouch down, put back the book, and shut the box.

If you decide to stay inside the van and hope the men walk by without discovering you, turn to page 33.

If you want to get out of the van through the front door, before the men open the door in the back, turn to page 51.

Riding in the race, you think, would only confuse things for you. After all, you are a reporter, and your job is to cover the race from beginning to end. Yet your reporter's instincts tell you that there is still a story behind the van.

After everyone leaves, and the street is again deserted, you decide to check out the van one more time. This time you get a lucky break. The door was left unlocked. Now you can look through the drawers and cabinets containing the bike equipment. You find the bike-racing rule book that you saw earlier. This time the book contains real rules. The coded pages are gone. This time the flashlight, although it looks the same as the one you saw before, is just an ordinary flashlight. Nothing unusual happens when you shine it on the book.

Were the men who offered you the chance to ride in the race really from the FBI? Whoever they were, they may have been trying to get you out of the way. The key to this whole mysterious business, you are sure, is still in the van. But if the men *are* the FBI, should you interfere?

Just as you are about to leave through the van's rear door, a man and a woman get into the front. You hide under a canvas in the rear. The van pulls away.

You are on the road for an hour and a half before the driver stops at a gas station. Neither the man nor the woman leaves the van. By the time the van stops again, another hour has passed. This time the man and the woman get out.

You try opening the rear door of the van, but it sticks. Finally, you get it open. You look around. The sign over the diner across the road says MIDVILLE MANOR DINER. You realize that you are over 150 miles from Watertown.

You call the *Dispatch* office from the diner and find out that the FBI is looking for you. You tell Mr. Sam what happened, and he tells you to wait there. One of the FBI agents will be there shortly to pick you up.

The man and the woman never come back to the van. You and the FBI agents suspect that they knew someone was keeping an eye on them, so they left town in a hurry. Though you are tired, you still manage to cover the bike race from the press bus the next day. Your story on the race is a good one, but you never do find out who those people in the mystery van were.

THE END

from page 6

Wheels has been in the bike business ever since he stopped racing. He knows most of the riders by their first names. When you tell him what you heard, he just laughs. Wheels walks to the front of the store and points to the men you just observed.

"Those guys are two of the craziest bike racers in the world," he says. "When I was riding, they used to pull all sorts of jokes. I think they know you're a reporter and just tried to play some tricks on you. That press badge you have on is a dead giveaway."

Wheels takes you outside the store to meet his two friends, Joe Burke and Ernie Mueller. Wheels introduces you as a friend and a local reporter.

"No hard feelings about our little joke, I hope," says Joe, with a grin.

You have to smile, too. Then Wheels reveals that he has been asked by the Clean and Sweet Soap Company to ride in the big race tomorrow. He says that he's in good shape.

"I'm not as race-wise as I was a few years ago," Wheels says, "but I can still beat you guys."

At the last minute, the soap company has decided to enter its own team to ride in the Watertown race. Now Wheels will compete against the powerful Slick Messenger team.

He tells you that some local riders have agreed to ride with him on the new team while other people from the area will work on the support team. After talking with his friends, Wheels takes you back to his shop and introduces you to Ed Leffel of the Clean and Sweet Soap Company. Wheels asks Ed to persuade you to ride in the race or at least to work on the support team.

Ed tells you that they have plenty of extra bikes you could use. Ed also says it would be a great opportunity for you to see the race as it actually happens. You agree that it's a rare opportunity for a reporter. But you wonder if you could make it the entire eighty-three miles.

If you decide to be part of the support team in the van, turn to page 70.

If you decide to ride in the race, turn to page 117.

It's just too risky to stay in the van. Still crouched down, you grab the door handle and in one motion twist it open and roll outside. But the van's inside lights go on as you slide to the ground. Startled, the two men rush to the front of the van.

"Got you," says one of them. "Just get in the van. Let's have a little talk."

While one of the men drives out of town, the other starts questioning you.

"Look, you're in big trouble if you don't tell us what you were doing in our van," the man says. "We'll call the police."

You tell them that you are a reporter for the local paper, gathering background information on the teams and on what the support vans do during the race.

"Sure you are," the man says. "And I'm the tooth fairy."

You realize that these people mean business. About five miles from the center of town, a limousine pulls up alongside you. You can see the grim faces of several men in the back seat. The driver motions the van to pull over. Then, following the limousine, the van turns down a dirt road.

A short distance down the dirt road, the two vehicles come to a stop. The back door of the limousine opens and a tall man emerges.

"What's your name?" he asks you. "Why were you snooping around the van?" You tell him what you told the first two men.

After a short silence, the tall man asks, "Would you be willing to forget about this incident for the sake of national security?"

If you decide to trust these men, turn to page 96.

If you don't trust them, turn to page 105.

from page 72

You drive by the van in the ditch but call in its position to the state police on the CB radio.

Soon you hear Al shouting encouragement to one of your riders. He tells the rider her speed and hands her an energy drink in a special container. You notice the sun is getting hotter, and some of the riders are slowing down.

Along the course, some riders have developed cramps in their legs and have parked at the side of the road to get a hasty massage from their trainers. Halfway through the race, you change positions in the van and help Harry change tires on two bikes.

Wheels makes good progress in the race. As he nears Snake Hill, he begins passing other riders. When you pass him some water, he smiles and tells you that he feels terrific. Then he speeds up again and passes more riders.

When Wheels hits Snake Hill, your van is only two hundred yards behind him. You see him start up the hill and disappear around a curve. When the van catches up again, Wheels is on the ground—it's his second accident of the day.

"A rider ahead of me hit a rock in the road," he tells you, "and everyone behind him got caught in the spill. You fellows had better get me a new bike. I can't use this one anymore."

While Al is preparing a new bike for Wheels, you bandage up the brave cyclist's scrapes. The crew works furiously to get Wheels's new bike ready. You really like being part of the team.

You and the crew cheer Wheels over the hill and follow him to the finish. Even though he doesn't win, Wheels is delighted that he finished the race.

You are now ready to write a story for the *Dispatch* about the support vans and their important role in the race. But when you walk near the judge's stand after the race, you hear some of the officials talking to the police. You overhear one of them say, "You mean the bank was robbed, and the criminals escaped in a vehicle disguised as a support van?"

Now you wonder if you should have checked out that brown van on the side of the road. It would have been dangerous, but what a story you might have had.

THE END

You go down to the police station and talk to Sergeant Granger. You have known him since you were little, so he listens carefully to your story.

"Well, maybe this mystery van is parked illegally in that alley," he says, and winks at you. "It's up to us to make sure we know who owns it."

You take him to the spot where the van was parked, but it is no longer there. As you get back into his patrol car, Sergeant Granger says that he will put out an alert on the van and bring in the driver for questioning.

"There's not much more that we can do," the sergeant says. "But if you see the van again, call me immediately."

Later that day you find a phone message on your desk at the paper. It says Sergeant Granger wants you to meet him at a restaurant on the riverfront. Maybe he found the mystery vehicle, you think. But when you get to the restaurant, it is closed and no one is around.

As you walk along the pier, a hand reaches out and grabs you. Two men tie you up and stuff you into the trunk of a car. They both speak English with a heavy foreign accent. After an uncomfortable hour's drive, they take you out of the trunk and carry you into a small cabin.

The leader, a man the others call Mr. J., is wearing sunglasses and an ash-colored hat. "Why were you snooping around my van today?" he asks.

After he repeats the question several times, you realize that you had better tell them something. You say that you are a reporter and wanted to interview the members of his racing team. The people in the cabin laugh.

"We know you're being paid by the CIA," says Mr. J.

You repeat yourself without success.

Later that night, they tie you securely to a small rowboat and push you downstream toward Watertown. Unfortunately, the boat gets tangled in a fallen tree. It could be a long time before you are found.

THE END

58

from page 43

After you've had time to think about it, you wonder why you ever volunteered to ride in the race. The only bike races that you've ever ridden in have been local ten-milers. You wonder if you can go the distance of the Great Watertown Race.

One of the FBI agents who recruited you introduces you to Wayne Durdeen, the agent in charge of the FBI team protecting the Contron plant.

"We really appreciate what you're doing," Durdeen tells you. "Don't wory about the race. You'll do fine." He takes you around the block to meet the team.

After introducing you to all the members of the support team, Durdeen introduces you to the other racer they've recruited from Watertown, Kate Powers. You've known Kate for a long time. She also used to ride in local races, but she injured herself about a year ago.

Kate greets you and tries to ease your nervousness.

"Before we talk tactics," she says, "I think we'd better get outfitted for the race."

Kate climbs into the gray van to get you a black, red, and silver Slick team jersey. She hands you the jersey and a pair of black racing shorts that have a suede seat. She finds you some gloves, shoes, and a safety helmet.

You go into the van and put on the uniform. Once you are in the racing uniform you feel strangely at ease, as though you're ready for anything.

Next, Kate takes you over to meet Scoot, whom you've already "met" on your own. Scoot is the chief mechanic for the team, but he is also an FBI agent. He is going to fit you for a bike. He puts you on a shiny blue and silver one. While Kate helps to steady the bike, Scoot adjusts the seat, the handlebars, and the gear-shift mechanism.

"Now you're ready to ride straight to the finish line without a hitch," says Scoot.

You take your new racing bike out for a short ride. It really is a smooth-riding machine. Compared to your own bike, this one seems like a rocket.

When you get back, you talk to Kate about strategy for the race.

"Don't worry about winning," she says. "Just plan on trying to finish the race. Drink plenty of fluids and keep your pace steady."

"Now," says Mr. Durdeen, "go home and get a good night's sleep. We'll give you a final briefing tomorrow morning."

The alarm clock seems to ring extra early the next morning. The racing van picks you up at 6:30 to take you to Cedarville for the start of the race.

Mr. Durdeen and the other agents brief you on what they expect you to do during the race. As you ride, your job is to spot suspicious people along the side of the road. Inside your helmet is a radio that allows you to send and receive messages from the van.

When you get to Cedarville, you sense the excitement. The starting area is a vivid sight with all the colorful bikes and racing jerseys.

You line up next to Kate. She winks at you without further greeting. Before you know it, the starting gun goes off. Everyone seems to fly right past you, but your custom-made racing bike makes it easy for you to pick up speed.

As you leave the Cedarville city limits, you go around a sharp curve. At a fork in the road just beyond the curve, about ten riders suddenly crash in a dangerous pile-up. As they go down, someone pushes you from behind! Your bike goes down, too. By the time you get back on your bike, everyone has passed you. You are dazed but, luckily, not hurt. You're not sure of the route, and Kate and the other riders are long gone.

To the right, the road seems to follow a wide river. You think you see hills to the left.

If you decide to go to the left, turn to page 27.

If you decide to take the right fork, turn to page 62.

from page 61

Right is right! You remember that the course follows the Willow River. In about thirty seconds, you catch up with the main body of cyclists. You have never ridden so fast on a bike before, but on this special one it seems almost easy.

As you shift gears to take a hill, you see Kate at your side. She is motioning to you to drink some water out of the bottle clamped on your bike frame. As you drink, you sense the rhythm of the pack of riders and how you are part of it. When you reach the top of the hill, you can see the race leaders at the bottom going around the bend in the road. Going downhill is easier, and very fast.

So far you have seen nothing suspicious. You know there are two electronics plants along this route. It's hard to understand why anyone would want to steal something in broad daylight during a bike race. You keep looking along the road for something that might be a clue. At about thirty-five miles into the race, you notice that one of the riders has a leaking water bottle.

You think it's odd that the rider doesn't see the leak, even though it's pouring out faster and faster. You find out too late that the bottle is leaking *oil*, not water. Several bikes ahead of you skid and crash, one after the other. Kate also takes a spill. You see the rider turn back and look at everyone sliding and falling on the road.

Quickly, you turn your bike to the side of the road and ride slowly on the gravel shoulder. Your quick thinking and good reflexes help you avoid the pile-up of bikes. You do not go down.

Turning on your helmet radio, you call Mr. Durdeen and tell him that the rider who caused the accident is wearing a red jersey with blue and gold stripes.

As you pedal harder than ever, you figure out why the rider chose this part of the race to spill the oil and cause the pile-up. Around the bend in the road is Starius Electronics, the leading supplier to the government of missile-guidance systems.

As spectators run toward the scene of the accident, you continue to follow the mystery rider. He is joined by another rider, and they are pointing toward the Starius plant. The second rider throws his water bottle toward the front gate. The two riders put on gas masks as blue smoke starts to rise from the bottle. Just then a brown van drives up to the gate. Six people get out of the van wearing gas masks, throwing more smoke bombs. They run into the plant, past the coughing, helpless security guards.

You call on your radio for help, but there is no answer.

If you want to wait for the FBI, turn to page 91.

If you decide to go into the plant on your own, turn to page 67.

from page 105

You agree to "join" the gang, but only if they let you stay in the van until after the race. They agree to this.

When you get back in the van, you wonder how you're ever going to explain this to Mr. Sam. After all, you were supposed to be covering the bike race.

After driving around the outskirts of Watertown, the men decide that they need something to eat. Packard asks you where there's a quiet roadside restaurant.

"The Gemini Diner is down the road at the next intersection," you tell him.

What you don't tell him is that Watertown's Sheriff Stryker, and his deputies, frequently have a late supper there after their shift is over. You know the sheriff pretty well from your work on the newspaper.

Packard drives the van up to the diner and parks for about five minutes. Then he sends one of his men inside to check the place out. In a moment, the man comes back and says, "It looks okay. Nobody is in there but a couple of old guys."

When you walk in with Packard and the rest of the men, you are disappointed. Neither the sheriff nor any of his deputies is there. When Leo, the owner of the diner, recognizes you with the group, he winks and rolls his eyes in the direction of the back booth. There you see Sheriff Stryker and Mr. Sam talking over a cup of coffee. When the waiter takes your order, you recognize him as one of the sheriff's deputies. You ask Packard if you can go to the washroom.

He says, "Sure, but I'll go along."

When you come out of the washroom, Packard is right behind you. "Keep moving quickly," he says. Suddenly there is a scuffle behind you. Sheriff Stryker and one of his men have Packard in handcuffs. When you get to the table, the rest of the men from PITA are being led out the door.

Outside, you meet Mr. Sam, "It was sure lucky that Sheriff Stryker saw you with those wanted men," he says. "Somebody else might not have recognized them. Tell me the whole story. Better than that, write it for the *Dispatch*. But first, let me buy you a good dinner!"

After eating two of Leo's best hamburgers, you go back with Mr. Sam to the newspaper office and write the story of the year for your paper.

THE END

There's no time to waste, you say to yourself. As you run into the plant you find yourself almost blinded by stinging blue smoke. You crouch down and crawl along as best you can. You hear shouting from around a corner. Following the sound, you approach a room labeled TOP SECRET—DO NOT ENTER. You try calling Mr. Durdeen on the radio, but there is still no answer.

Just then, two men wearing gas masks call out to you, "Halt, or we'll shoot."

The two men grab you and haul you out of the plant. They take you to a van, tie you up, and drive away. You are blindfolded and gagged. After driving about three hours, they pull you from the van and tie you to a tree near the highway.

It will be dusk soon. Your only hope is that someone will find you before dark.

THE END

68

from page 80

Once the tank is filled, the men head the van back toward the racecourse. To make conversation, you ask them where their riders are. They tell you that four got hurt and only two are still in the race.

When you ask them what colors their team wears, one man says, "Green and yellow," and at the same time another says, "Blue and gray." They've obviously blundered. They try to cover it up by saying they used to wear green and yellow; now it's blue and gray.

Your only chance to get home safely now is to play along—if it isn't already too late. You hope the bank robbers don't decide that their blunder has been obvious to you, and that now you know too much.

When the van gets back on the race route, it picks up speed. Since vans drive faster than bikes, you soon catch up to the pack. Suddenly you spot the Clean and Sweet van parked on the side of the road, fixing a team member's bike. Thinking quickly, you ask to be dropped off by your team's van. The men seem glad to let you out.

You're relieved when the mystery van pulls away and rides off ahead of all the racers. You tell Al what happened, and ask him to use your van's CB radio to call the police.

"Bank robbers posing as members of a bike-racing team?" says Doc. "That's pretty hard to believe."

Al tries calling on the CB radio, but all you get is a great deal of static. Then the radio seems to go dead. Harry says it must be the hills the van is passing through.

When you finally catch up to Wheels again, the sweat is pouring through the white racing cap that covers his leather helmet. He says that he is tired but has enough energy left to finish the race.

When the van stops to repair another rider's tire, you remember that your tape recorder has been on. You take out the tape and replace it with a new one.

You look into the rearview mirror and see that Harry and Doc are talking to Al. Then they point toward you.

"What's up, guys?" you ask.

"Let's get to the finish line. We think one of our best riders is in trouble ahead."

At that point you see the wire from the CB radio hanging down, disconnected from the dashboard. When you show Doc the wire, he says that someone must have kicked it. Something seems funny about the three men since you returned to the van. The finish line is now only moments away.

If you want to check on your teammates after you reach the finish line, turn to page 74.

If you would rather talk to Mr. Sam when you get to the finish, turn to page 85.

from page 50

You think you might get the best story on the race while riding in the support van. The morning of the race, you meet the support crew in Cedarville. The van is freshly painted in the colors of the Clean and Sweet Soap Company: bright green and sea blue. Wheels is there, along with the bike mechanics, Harry and Doc. Wheels tells them that you've volunteered to help them in the van.

The two mechanics are making some last-minute adjustments on some bikes. All of your team's riders look tense. Some are on the ground doing stretching exercises. Others are fidgeting with their bicycles, making some adjustments of their own.

Doc comes over and introduces you to Al, who helps coach the team. Al tells you that he was never a great rider, but he found that he could do a good job training riders. He also says that he works full time for the soap company. Then he takes you inside the van and shows you where everything is.

Ten bike frames are mounted on the roof of the van. Inside, you see twelve extra wheels with quick-release levers. Al explains that the extra wheels and bikes are used as spares in emergencies. During a race, tires are changed in seconds, or whole bikes are quickly substituted if the riders need them. Also inside the van are bins full of spare parts. Bike chains and lubricating oil sit alongside baskets of fruit and special plastic bottles filled with liquids. The food and the special liquids are used to give the riders energy, especially on hot days.

Al has an electric megaphone that he will use during the race to communicate with the riders. When the race begins, it will be your job to help pass extra drinks to the riders. Al will keep the riders informed about their positions in the race while Doc and Harry will be ready to repair the team's bikes.

Just before the race begins, you remember the tape recorder Mr. Sam gave you. You turn it on to record what is going on inside the van, to help you remember details for your story on the race.

As the gun goes off, everyone gets into the van. There appears to be all sorts of commotion as the racers jockey for position and the support vehicles quickly set out to follow them. Police cars with their sirens on lead the way. As you head out of town, you see a brown van trailing you. It has darkened windows and only a few bikes on top.

The brown van picks up speed and passes yours. You barely see the driver. You ask Doc what team's van that was. He doesn't know.

About fifteen miles into the race, you see Wheels standing on the side of the road.

"Some guys in a brown van sideswiped me," he says when you stop to help him.

You quickly give Wheels a new bike and clean the scrape on his leg. Why are those guys in the brown van in such a hurry? Wheels gets back into the race. He is almost last now, but at least he is still riding.

As you drive farther up the road, you see the brown van stuck in a ditch. Should you stop to help, or keep driving?

If you think your van should stop to help them, turn to page 78.

If your team decides not to stop, turn to page 54.

You suspect that the three men in your van may somehow be involved in the bank robbery. When you get to the finish line, you go over to the officials' tent to look up Ed Leffel of the Clean and Sweet Soap Company. You tell him about the van in the ditch and the money bag you saw in the van. And you tell him your suspicion that his team may also have been involved in the bank robbery.

Mr. Leffel tells you that his crew has been racing together for a long time, and that Al works for the company in a responsible position. "You may have been reading too many detective stories," he says with a smile. "Your suspicion is understandable, but you're wrong about the team being in on the robbery." You are still not convinced, but you don't say anything else to Mr. Leffel. You decide to go talk to Watertown's sheriff.

Before you can leave, Harry and Doc ask you to help them put away the equipment in the van. They offer you a cool drink. In a moment, you see everything spinning.

You wake up six hours later. Wheels helps you get to the sheriff's office, and you tell what happened. After calling the soap company, the sheriff tells you that Al has suddenly quit the team and left town. Wheels tells you he heard that the two mechanics, Doc and Harry, just caught a plane to Europe, where they've found work.

When you and the sheriff question Ed Leffel, he tells you that Al won the lottery and moved to California. You confirm this when you check the paper. Whatever the mystery is, you'll never get to the bottom of it.

THE END

from page 80

You decide you must call the police, but you ought to divert the attention of the men in the van. Telling them that you need some air, you go to the washroom. You come out after a few minutes, only to find that the van is gone.

"They told me to tell you that they couldn't wait," the attendant says. "They had to get back to the bike race."

You call the police, and they arrive in five minutes. You tell them your story about the van and the money bag. The station attendant shows the police which way the van was headed. The state trooper in charge radios an alert on the van.

Then the police give you a ride to the finish line. By this time, the race is over. A tired but happy Wheels Wilson spots you and tells you that you missed an exciting finish. Ten riders had a chance to win the race. It was a furious sprint over the last half mile, and a young rider from Spain won the race by only a foot. Wheels says, "I wasn't in good enough shape to be in the lead group, but I'm still pleased with how I rode today."

You walk over to see the trophies and medals being awarded. In the back of the awards platform is the mysterious brown van! You run over to see if there is anyone in it. It is completely empty. Only the bikes are on top.

After everyone leaves, no one returns to pick up the van. You call the police again. After several days of watching the van, nothing happens.

Later in the month, you read about the capture of the bank robbers in Florida. You are glad they were arrested, but you wish you could have been the one who caught them.

THE END

from page 72

Your van pulls off the road ahead of the brown van. Al says he'll go with you and see if he can give them a hand. When you get to the van, two men come out and greet you.

"Can we help you?" you say.

They accept your offer and ask you and Al to give them a push. You get the van out of the ditch. The two men thank you and ask where they can buy some gasoline. You tell them that the nearest gas station is right down the road. You suspect something, though. The only way to find out what they're up to is to stay with them. So you say, "I'll show you."

"I'd better get back to the race," Al says, as he goes to get back into his van. "See you afterwards."

You get into the back of the brown van. There are two other men inside. You realize too late that anyone in a support van should have had enough gas to last a whole race. And when you look around inside, you don't see any riding gear. Now you're really on the alert.

You spot what appears to be a rag on the floor. When the men are not looking, you pick it up and see that it's a bag, with the words PROPERTY OF CEDARVILLE BANK printed on it. It's an empty money bag. You say nothing and try to remain casual and calm.

One of the men suddenly calls to you from the front of the van, "Which way is the gas station?" You tell them to drive up the road and turn right at the first intersection.

As you approach the gas station, the van's radio stops playing music, and a special bulletin is announced: "The Cedarville Bank was robbed early this morning. It appears that a gang of robbers dug their way through the floor of the main storage vault and made off with over five hundred thousand dollars. There have been no clues as to where the robbers fled or how they made their getaway." The two men in the back of the van look at each other but don't say a word.

Just as the music comes back on the radio, the van pulls into the gas station. The leader of the group puts on sunglasses and gets out. He tells the attendant to fill 'er up. Then he goes over to a phone booth and makes a call. You see him smiling as he is talking.

If you decide to keep acting casual, turn to page 68.

If you decide to get out of the van, too, and find a way to make a call to the police, turn to page 76.

from page 104

You decide to stay with Wheels and wait for the van.

"The last time I was in this race, I had a real chance to win it all," Wheels tells you. "But it was right here that I got a flat. This hill must be jinxed for me."

Your support van comes along in about two minutes and the crew assists Wheels. He isn't really hurt, just scraped up and bruised a little. The crew gives him a new bike, and you rejoin the race together.

From the top of the hill, you can see the leaders and the rest of the riders ahead. Nothing seems unusual at the Contron Electronics plant. As you go down the hill, the stiffness in your legs begins to go away. You pass a few riders, mostly stragglers, who look pretty tired.

By the time you and Wheels hit the finish line, most of the spectators and racers are at the nearby presentation ceremonies. You can see the winner. He is wearing a jersey that says SONIC SPEEDERS. Wheels turns to you and tells you that the Sonic Speeders must be a new team. He's never heard of them before.

Later in the day, you get back to the newspaper office to write your firsthand account of the race. Ed Leffel of the soap company had given you a press release about the winners. The release says the winner was an unknown rider from Cedarville.

On a hunch, you phone Super Cycles, Inc., and find that the phone has been disconnected. You are almost certain that there is a connection between the Sonic Speeders and Super Cycles, Inc., but you can't figure it out. When you tell Mr. Sam about it, he says to stick to the facts about the race and finish your story.

You wish you had been able to unravel the mystery. But all you can do now is write your story for the *Dispatch* about how a rider with no previous cycling experience came out of nowhere to win the race. On one last hunch, you call the operator for the winner's number. The operator tells you that no such person lives in Cedarville. It seems as if the Sonic Speeders have pulled a fast one. But you may never find out what they did.

THE END

from page 105

You refuse to join Packard, even though you may be placing your life in greater danger. In fact, as soon as you say no, he ties you up and puts you in the back of the van. Two of the men drive off in the limousine. Packard and the rest of the PITA scientists get in the van and drive back onto the main road. You try your best to remain calm.

After about an hour of traveling through the outskirts of Watertown, the van turns off the highway onto a dirt road. Packard tells the others, "We'd better stay here for the night. Then we can pay a visit to Contron at around five A.M." When he opens the van doors, you can see that you are not far from Snake Hill. That means you are even closer to Contron Electronics.

The scientists go to sleep. Soon all is quiet except for the sound of crickets. Time passes slowly. You must have fallen asleep, because you are suddenly aware of someone shaking your arm. One of the scientists is awake. "Quickly!" he whispers.

He cuts your ropes and walks off quietly into the woods. Apparently this is one scientist who is having second thoughts about committing sabotage.

You don't waste a second in deciding what to do. You walk, then run quietly along the dirt road toward the highway.

You hope a car will pick you up soon. With any luck, you can call the Watertown police and stop the criminals before it is too late.

THE END

from page 69

When you see Mr. Sam after the race, you tell him your suspicions about the men in the two vans. You ask him if you are imagining too much. He says that good reporters have to be expert observers.

"You have to look at everything from all angles," he says. "Try to recall the events as they happened."

You start by telling him how the Clean and Sweet support team showed you around their van this morning. Then Al showed you what to do during the race. Suddenly you remember that you turned on the tape recorder at the start of the race. You rewind the tape and play it for Mr. Sam.

Everything you told him about the race is confirmed by the tape, until the point where your van stopped to help the brown van in the ditch. When you and Al left the van, the tape picked up the conversation between Doc and Harry.

"When those two start pushing the van out of the mud," Doc says on the tape, "you go around the side and pick up the suitcase with the money. I'll stay here and watch out for trouble."

A few minutes go by on the tape before you hear Harry say, "I got it and put it in the tool cases."

At that moment the tape ends.

"I think you've got a big story," says Mr. Sam. "We'd better call Sheriff Stryker."

When the sheriff arrives at the news office, you repeat your story and play him the tape. After listening to the tape, the sheriff asks you to go with him to check out the vans. First he calls his office for some backup deputies.

You find Harry and Doc inside their van, cleaning up the gear from the race. They look startled to see the sheriff with you.

Doc asks the sheriff what's wrong. Stryker tells them he wants to hear their story on what happened with the brown van. Harry and Doc repeat the same story of how you and Al helped get the van out of the ditch.

Then the sheriff notices two large tool cases near the rear of the van. He asks the mechanics to open them up. They start to run, but it's too late. Two of the sheriff's deputies grab them.

When the two men are brought to jail, they confess to masterminding the robbery. They tell the sheriff that Al wasn't in on the robbery. The actual

crime took place early in the morning, before the start of the race. Four people used the brown van to pull off the bank robbery. The four are arrested an hour after Harry and Doc confess. What they hadn't planned on was that you would be there with your tape recorder.

You have solved the mystery at the bike race.

THE END

Knowing Mr. Sam often works late, you hurry back to the *Dispatch* office and tell him what you have just witnessed. You tell him your suspicion that the electronics plant and its AMIGS project—whatever that is—might be in danger. But neither of you can figure out how the men would use the bike race in their plan.

Mr. Sam places a call to a friend of his in Washington, D.C. He tells his friend what you told him, then he hangs up.

"He'll call us back in a few minutes," says Mr. Sam.

Five minutes later, the phone rings. Your boss tells you to pick up the extension phone and listen.

The woman at the other end seems excited.

"You may have stumbled onto something important," the woman says, "and you'd better be careful about it. Sam, you always knew how to dig out the exclusive stories, but this time it just has to stay quiet. I've passed this information on to the chief. He says to tell you that our people need silence and cooperation in this. Sam, you know that national security is at stake."

After she hangs up, Mr. Sam tells you, "It sounds like we'd better just cover the race. The government wants to keep this quiet." He then tries to explain what his Washington friend was talking about.

The next morning the mysterious van has vanished, and there are extra security guards around the electronics plant. When you cover the race from the press truck, you pass by the plant and wonder what's really going on in there.

The FBI handles the situation so well that not a word gets out. The authorities have you and Mr. Sam to thank for uncovering the plot. As a citizen, you're pleased about what you've done. But as a reporter, you just wish you knew a little more about the foiled plot.

THE END

You call the FBI for help. Mr. Durdeen comes on the radio, and you tell him what's happening. As you are talking, several gunshots ring out. One of the plant's security officers has been hit and is lying on the ground.

"I'm going in there to help the security guard," you tell Mr. Durdeen.

You run quickly to the guard, who's been wounded in the right arm.

"Stop them," says the guard. "Whatever they're after can't get into the wrong hands. Here, take my pistol. Try to stop them, or it'll be too late."

You radio a description of the van as it starts to pull away from the plant. With the guard's gun, you take aim at the van and fire three shots. One of the bullets punctures the van's front tire!

The van screeches to a stop, and seven people get out. Just then, Mr. Durdeen's van pulls up alongside the van. The FBI agents, backed by state police, arrest the thieves.

"Wait a minute," you say to yourself. "Eight men went into the plant. Now there are only seven."

You notice that only one of the seven men is wearing bike-racing clothes. The other rider must have slipped away unnoticed in all the commotion.

You run back for your bike, climb aboard, and start pedaling hard toward the finish. From the top of the hill you can see the rest of the racers heading toward Watertown. You see way behind them a rider wearing a red jersey with blue and gold stripes. It must be the rider who entered the plant! You radio Mr. Durdeen and tell him where the rider is headed. In one minute, cars from the state police pull alongside the rider and arrest him.

When you finally get to the finish line, you see Mr. Sam waiting for you with Mr. Durdeen.

"Since you were so far behind, we thought you needed a cheering section at the finish line," says Mr. Sam. "You certainly deserve some kind of award. That was some way to get a story!"

THE END

from page 122

You ride out to the plant on your motorbike. As you approach Snake Hill, you see the gray, almost windowless plant, the high barbed-wire fence, and No Trespassing signs around it.

When you reach the top of the hill, you realize that from this vantage point you can see miles down the road in both directions. As you look back over your shoulder, you see that this would be a great place to watch a key part of the race. Suddenly, as you pass in front of the plant entrance, you hit a rock in the road. Your motorbike goes out of control, and you fall to the ground.

A uniformed guard leaves his post at the gate. He runs over to you and helps you to your feet.

"That's a pretty nasty scrape you have on your leg," he says. "You'd better come inside and let our first-aid people look at it."

He puts your bike in the guard shack and helps you inside. When you get to the main door of the plant, you see nothing but blank walls and another guard. There are no offices or machinery rooms in sight.

In the first-aid room, the company nurse cleans your scrape and applies some medicine. To make conversation, she asks what brought you to the area.

"I'm working on a story about the bike race for the *Dispatch*," you say.

"Oh," she says. "That's the race that comes by here every year, isn't it?"

Then she says something that you find interesting.

"You know, for the last three days I've seen a strange-looking gray van following cyclists up the hill. It always stops or slows down when it gets near the plant. Yesterday I saw a cyclist on the road without his bike. He was wearing funny-looking shoes with a red design on them."

Is this just a coincidence? Somehow, you doubt it.

If you decide to ask the nurse to take you to the plant security manager's office, turn to page 98.

If you want to get Mr. Sam's help to find out more about the van, turn to page 40.

from page 53

Deciding to trust these men, you tell the tall man that you'll forget about the incident only if he tells you what is really going on.

No one says a word. The whole group just stares at you.

"All right," the man finally says. "We'll give you most of the story, but for the sake of national security, I have to leave out some of the details." He shows you his badge and identification card. His name is John Packard and he is a member of the FBI.

Mr. Packard explains that the FBI has been following a group of bike riders around the country. These riders have used races as a cover to spy on our national-defense system. The riders are equipped with special cameras and electronic gear that let them monitor our military installations and secret plants. Since there are two defense plants in this area, this race is the perfect place and time to catch the riders in the act of spying. You also learn that the riders have taken longer-than-usual rides around the Air Force base on the other side of Watertown.

You ask Mr. Packard if you can still cover the race for the *Dispatch*. You tell him that when the spies are captured, you would like to write the story.

"Sure. After they're captured, it would be perfectly all right," Mr. Packard says.

Mr. Packard drives you back to the news office and asks you to call your boss, Mr. Sam, at home. When Mr. Sam arrives at the office, Mr. Packard explains the situation and how important it is to remain silent about the spies for now. "If word of our investigation reached them, they would either flee the country or just disappear," says the agent. "We need to have them in the open, so we can see who their contacts are. This way we can get the whole ring of spies."

After Mr. Packard leaves, Mr. Sam smiles and says, "You certainly have a nose for news. You can cover the entire story for the *Dispatch* as soon as the spies are under arrest."

You're going to have quite a scoop on all the big-city newspapers.

THE END

Kurt Murray is the security manager at Contron. A former FBI agent, he has been with the electronics company since it moved to Watertown three years ago. You tell Mr. Murray what you heard in town and what the company nurse told you about the van she has been seeing.

Mr. Murray gives you a strange look. Then he says, "Look, we've had our eyes on those two since they came to town. This plant makes highly classified electronics gear for the government. It's my job to see that every suspicious character who comes anywhere near here is checked out completely. I called in their descriptions to Washington. The FBI sent back detailed reports. These fellows are just what they claim to be—bike riders and mechanics."

Mr. Murray picks up the reports he has on the same two men that you saw in town. You get a glimpse of their pictures—on bikes. He tells you that the two men must have just been checking out the hill in preparation for the race. They need to know how steep it is on both sides, so their team will have a better idea of how hard it's going to be to climb it.

You tell Mr. Murray about the strange red design on the riders' shoes. "That's a special kind of shoe that's made in the Orient," he answers. "You don't see too many around here."

"I still think something is going on that's connected with this plant and the race," you tell Mr. Murray.

"Well, I can't find a shred of evidence to support your suspicion," says Mr. Murray. "I think you'd better get back to town and start worrying about how you're going to cover the race."

If you think you should follow his advice and start covering the race, turn to page 111.

If you think you should continue to investigate on your own, turn to page 11.

100

from page 120

You hide around the corner from the blue van so you won't be seen. In an hour, four men come out of a doorway carrying what looks like a body dressed in a bike-racing outfit. They all get into the van and drive away. It is darker now, so you can't even see the license-plate number.

The night security guard of the Tobor Industries building seems frightened when you walk through the side door. "What do you want?" he says. "You came in here so quietly, you scared me half to death."

You apologize and explain that you're a reporter working on a special story. You are trying to find out who the men were that came out the door. You also ask, "Who were they carrying?"

"They said it was just one of their riders who wasn't feeling well," he says. "Those fellows are in the import business, and they have their own cycling team for tomorrow's race.

"Bicycles are the only thing I've ever seen in their office," the guard continues. "They're fairly new tenants and keep to themselves. They usually work very late at night. I guess it would be all right if you want to see their office."

He lets you look through the glass of their office door, which bears the words SUPER CYCLES, INC. The office is plain and neat. It looks almost unused.

You figure that whatever these guys are up to, it isn't going to happen around the office. You head for home to get some sleep for the big race tomorrow.

Early the next morning, Wheels picks you up to drive to Cedarville for the start of the race. The sun is starting to come up, and the weather forecast predicts a hot, humid day. You feel rested but still a little uneasy about the people in the mysterious blue van. As you drive from the finish to the start, Wheels begins to tell you about the course. You have been over this road many times on your bike, but this time Wheels makes it sound and look different. He points out the curves, the narrow stretches, the downhills, and the grinding uphills.

"Take your time," he keeps reminding you. "Don't attack the course until the very end. On a day like this, you can burn yourself out quickly. Just stay right behind me and I'll pull you through with flying colors."

When you get to the Clean and Sweet van at the starting line in Cedarville, you spot the blue van parked down a side street. It has several bikes on the roof and a sign on the side that reads SONIC SPEEDERS.

You and Wheels find your bikes all ready to go. You're in the middle of the pack when the starting gun goes off. It is mass confusion, but you find yourself on Wheels' tail as the pack leaves Cedarville.

During the first twenty miles, you feel strong and smooth. Then the pace quickens, and Wheels moves ahead of you by at least three hundred yards. By the time you reach the forty-five-mile mark, you realize that you must be riding at a twenty-four-mile-per-hour pace. You are pleased with your performance so far, but your legs are starting to feel the strain, and you're only halfway through the race.

Your support van drives up beside you, and one of the people inside hands you a banana and some water. (Bananas give you energy and help prevent muscle cramps.) The sun is getting hotter as you head for the flat roads that lead up to Snake Hill. Wheels has told you many times that this hill is where the race is won or lost. It is three miles of winding, steep, uphill climbing. The Contron Electronics plant is at the top of the hill.

As you hit Snake Hill, you see the Sonic Speeders van as it passes you. After the first mile, your legs start to cramp and tire. As you round a steep incline, you see some rocks in the road and a rider down on the side of the road. It's Wheels! You pull over to help him, and ask what happened.

"When I turned the curve, four huge rocks came down through the trees and caught my front wheel," he says. "I'm all right, but my bike is broken. I'll just wait for the van to come with a new bike; then I'll join you at the finish line. Don't wait for me. It's your first big race."

Wheels is your teammate, and you don't want to leave him alone, but you *can* finish the race—it's only ten more miles to Watertown.

If you decide to stay with Wheels and wait for the team van, turn to page 81.

If you decide to go ahead and finish the race, turn to page 107.

Even though you may be risking your life, you come right out and tell the man that it would be hard for you to forget what has happened.

The man grabs you by the collar and looks into your eyes. "I like someone who has principles," he says. "Since you're honest with us, we'll be honest with you: My name is Packard. We're scientists, and we want to get even with Contron Electronics because we lost a big contract to them. It cost all of us our jobs. We were with the PITA Corportation. Contron played dirty, and now we want to get even.

"We don't want to hurt people," Packard continues. "We just want to fix it so that Contron can't develop their anti-gravity missile-guidance system. With the equipment in our van, we can delay the AMIGS operation at least two years."

You've heard about AMIGS. This is important information that the government should know about. You've got to escape, but how?

"Look," says Packard, "you can work with us or be our prisoner. It's completely up to you."

If you decide to play along and say you will work with them, turn to page 64.

If you refuse to cooperate, turn to page 83.

Wheels assures you that he'll be all right. You hop on your bike and struggle up Snake Hill. You have only ten miles to go. It's getting hotter, and your body is really starting to ache. Everything seems okay at the plant. On your way down the other side of the hill, you catch up with the main body of cyclists, but you are still in the rear.

As you approach the last two miles of the race, you look over your shoulder and spot Wheels behind you, on a new bike. He's not waving to you or saying anything. That's unusual for Wheels. And you can't figure out how he has so much energy at this point in the race, especially after his accident. He's really coming on strong.

In less than a minute, he passes you. He doesn't say a word. He's not even sweating!

Wheels keeps moving—past practically everyone in the race—and then starts to pass the breakaway group. You may be seeing one of the greatest racing comebacks ever. It's a superhuman effort. Yet something seems very wrong to you.

Wheels starts to pass the leaders and pulls in front of them by fifty yards. You cheer when you see him take the lead. When the race gets into the center of town, you can hear the spectators' wild cheers, especially when Wheels hits the finish. Everyone loves it when a local competitor does well.

Ten minutes after you finish, you see Wheels standing alone—by the blue van. You run up to greet him, and he waves at you. The usually talkative Wheels says only one word: "Hi." Now you know what's wrong.

Quickly you take one of the CB radios from the Sonic Speeders van and cross some wires on the inside. In thirty seconds Wheels' entire body is smoking. You can't believe it, but it's right before your eyes.

"What are you doing?" yells Ed Leffel of the Clean and Sweet Soap Company as he hurries over to you.

You call out to Watertown's Sheriff Stryker and tell him to arrest Ed Leffel. The sheriff says that you had better explain yourself. Ed Leffel says angrily, "Are you crazy?"

You walk over to Wheels, who is still smoking, and push him to the ground. Wheels falls apart into thousands of intricate electronic parts—a robot!

"How did you figure that out?" asks the sheriff.

You tell him that it hit you just after you saw Wheels pass you in the race. You noticed something odd about Wheels—he wasn't sweating! "In this kind of weather he should have been soaked. Then I remembered seeing a book on robots in the Super Cycles office. I put two and two together."

Pointing to the blue van, you tell the sheriff that the real Wheels should be inside. Sure enough, you find the real Wheels bound and gagged on the floor of the van. After a quick conversation with you, Sheriff Stryker arrests Ed Leffel and takes him to jail. After you free Wheels, he thanks you, then asks, "Why Ed Leffel?"

"I did some checking on my own, with some of the reporters on the *Dispatch*," you say. "They knew that Mr. Leffel has had some serious money problems lately. He had a lot of gambling debts, and he bet that you would win this race. I found out from the town clerk that he rented space in the Tobor office building, where they build robots for industry. He stole one of the humanoid prototypes from the Tobor company and had him shaped to look like you. Mr. Leffel promised the people from Tobor who helped him a lot of money when his 'Wheels' won the race."

Then you tell him that the blue van probably followed you two last night to see how Wheels rode his bike, so Leffel and his partners could program the robot.

You've solved the mystery at the bike race.

THE END

Suspecting something may have happened to the other van, you tell Mr. Slick about the strange man you saw talking to Carl before the race.

But the company president doesn't seem concerned. "Don't worry about Willy," he tells you. "Everyone thinks Willy is a bit strange. He runs the other van. Willy was probably getting Carl a little nervous before the race. Carl's a nervous type anyway."

Just then the van slows down. The driver pulls off the road and turns to Mr. Slick. "Rear tire is flat," he says.

Everyone gets out of the van and looks at the flat. It takes about fifteen minutes to change the tire. By the time the van is back on the road, it's too late to see the riders climb the tough Snake Hill. Mr. Slick tells the driver to take a shortcut down a side road. The van gets to Watertown just in time for the end of the race.

You have missed seeing Joseph cross the finish line first. Carl, you find out, had a flat tire of his own on the other side of Snake Hill. Willy helped him change it, but not in enough time to finish high in the standings.

After the awards ceremony, you thank Mr. Slick and head back to the paper to write your story. A flat story about flat tires. Well, maybe next year.

THE END

You take Mr. Murray's advice and go back to the newspaper office to work on your race story. You seem to have covered a lot of ground without getting any solid facts. When you get to the paper, you find Mr. Sam at his desk with a copy of a weekly newsmagazine.

"See this story on Cedric Wheyworth?" he asks. "It seems that he might be in town this week. He secretly slipped into the Contron plant in what appeared to be a Slick Messenger Service van. He must be up at the plant right now. Did you see anything when you were up there?"

You play back for Mr. Sam your recording of the conversation you just had with Mr. Murray of Contron. "Well," he says, "I think he gave you a fast one. Better get some more material on the race. That's the only story we'll be able to cover. Whatever Wheyworth's up to, we'll never be able to figure it out.

"Cedric Wheyworth is one of those electronic geniuses who works in almost total secrecy," Mr. Sam continues. "One time he had his whole company fooled. It's reported that he worked on a sensitive project for over a month at his secret desert laboratory. Only his secretary knew he was gone. When anyone approached Wheyworth's office, his secretary used a remote-control switch to turn on a tape recording that played his voice talking on the telephone. No one ever suspected he was away from his office.

"Now with all of the security at the Contron plant, we'll never find out if he's in town. You'd better stick with your race story. A half hour ago I saw Joseph Romanov, the favorite to win this year's race, on his way to the bike shop with some of his teammates. Why don't you go over there and see if you can get an interview with him?" says Mr. Sam.

When you get to the bike shop, Joseph and his teammates are out in the parking lot with their support van. Joseph is glad to talk to you and to show you the extra-light, incredibly fast bike with which he hopes to win tomorrow's race. You tell him of your interest in racing, and the racing experiences you've had. He suggests that you think about joining a team for next year's race.

"Right now," you tell Joseph, "I'm thinking only about covering this race for the paper. I know it's going to be a great one, and I want to do the best story I can. Thanks for your help."

The next day, you follow the racers on your motorbike. You catch glimpses of Joseph, who is riding with the leaders. He sees you and gives you a quick wave, then surges into the lead. At the top of Snake Hill, you can see Contron Electronics, with all of the extra security around it. Is the security just because of the race, or is Cedric Wheyworth really there?

Joseph holds the lead and wins the race by thirty seconds. After all of his friends and teammates congratulate him, you walk over and shake his hand. "I knew that my bike would hold up all right," he says. "Next year, I'll help you put one together just like mine. Then I can help you train for the next Watertown race."

You may never find out about the mysterious Cedric Wheyworth, but your investigation brought you something better: a great story on the race, and a coach who will help you prepare for next year's competition.

THE END

114

from page 23

When you reenter the store, Wheels is about to close his shop for the day. There are only a few customers left inside. Wheels comes over to you and asks you more about the FBI agent, Martin Hooper. You tell him about the thefts from the plant, and that Agent Hooper has been assigned to find out who has been stealing the electronics parts.

"You know," Wheels says, "those two men were acting a bit strange. They came into the store and looked around, then asked a lot of questions about the mileage out to Snake Hill, where the plant is. I just wonder if those guys were really bike fans."

You call Agent Hooper and tell him what you heard from Wheels. He thanks you for the information and asks you to keep a lookout for the van and the two men.

Just as you hang up, you see the two men drive past Wheels' store in a green van. Could they have switched vans? You run back to phone Agent Hooper, but the line is busy.

You could try to follow them on your motorbike. You try calling Agent Hooper again, but the line is still busy.

You run out to your motorbike, but the van is gone. Recalling what Wheels told you about the men and their questions about Snake Hill, you decide to drive out there before it gets dark.

When you get to the top of the hill, the sun has already gone down. Looking around carefully, you see what you think might be the green van. It's hidden off the road about three hundred yards from the plant. Cautiously, you walk down the hill and try to see if there is anyone around. You spot three people cooking around a campfire. One of them looks like one of the men you saw in front of Wheels' store.

You walk back to your bike and head over to the plant gate. You ask the guard if you can make an emergency phone call. When you call Mr. Hooper, you tell him that you may have spotted the men from the mystery van. He tells you to wait for him at the gate.

Mr. Hooper arrives ten minutes later and asks you to lead him to the van. You walk with him back down the trail.

"You stay here," Mr. Hooper says, "and if I get in any trouble, call the police."

He walks up to the fire. You see him talking to four people, not three. And two of them are women. Soon you hear them all laughing. After a few minutes, he shakes hands with them and comes back up the trail.

He smiles when he sees you, and says, "Those *were* the same men you saw in front of the bike store this morning. They're camping here with their wives.

They had read about the Watertown race in a magazine, and since they were going to be near here on vacation, they decided to camp here to see the race. They say their unusual shoes are European bike-racing shoes; they just wear them because they're bike-racing fans. And they say they just happened to be standing next to the Slick van this morning. This green van is theirs."

Mr. Hooper tell you that in his job he has to follow up every lead. "I'm still grateful for your help," he says. "This might have been important. I'm still going to check out their story."

Later that night Hooper calls FBI headquarters to run a check on the campers. He calls you the next morning to thank you.

"It seems that the time they said they left home could not possibly put them in Watertown as fast as they told me," he says to you. "We're going to watch them closely without letting them know we're suspicious. This lead just may be the break we need to solve the case of the missing microchips. Keep up the good work, and thank you again for your help."

THE END

from page 50

You decide to ride in the race. Wheels is delighted. He congratulates you and takes you to the back of the store.

"Now I'm going to make you look like a real bike rider," he says.

He tosses you a green and blue jersey and a pair of racing shorts. Then he brings out some new riding shoes. One pair has the strange red emblem that you saw earlier. He says that these are a new brand that the riders say are more comfortable and more durable. You tell him that you would prefer to wear your own riding shoes.

Then Wheels offers you a choice between two kinds of racing helmets. One is solid white plastic, the other is made of leather with strips of foam inside. You pick the solid white one. He also gives you some leather gloves without fingers. Wheels then takes you into the repair shop and tells his best mechanic to fix you up with a new bike for the race.

Wheels and his assistant, Lewis, ask you to sit on one of the bikes already on a rack. Then they ask you your weight. After you pedal on the stand for a few minutes, Lewis measures various parts of your body.

Wheels explains that they are getting you the right "setup." After measuring you and calculating all the information, they will customize a bike for you. Lewis says it will take only two hours to put everything together.

When you come back to the store in two hours, Lewis has ready not only one bike but a duplicate one in case you have an accident. He tells you to take a test ride on each one. Wheels comes into the shop and asks you to ride with him and "loosen up a little."

You are amazed at how fast and easy the new bike rides. This is the finest piece of machinery you have ever ridden. Wheels tells you to follow him down a back road. It has gotten quite dark outside, though, and you are worried about running into something.

Wheels starts to pick up speed and disappears around a corner. When you turn the corner, you can see him about fifty yards ahead, being followed by a blue van. When you get up to the van, it slows down to let you pass, then stops, turns around, and heads back to town.

When you catch up to Wheels, you ask him if he knows who was in the van.

"No," he says, "but I felt they were watching me. I have no idea who they were."

When you head back to the shop, you see the same blue van parked on a side street. There are two men sitting in the front seat and one in the rear. When you ride past the van, you are shocked by something you see inside. You got only a brief glimpse, but you think the man in the back of the van looked like Wheels' twin brother, bike shirt and all. You park your bike, walk into the shop, and tell Wheels what you just saw.

"But I don't have a twin," Wheels says, "or, for that matter, a brother!"

Both of you walk out to find the van, but it has driven away. Something's up, but what? On your way home, you spot the van parked in an alley.

If you decide to take a closer look at the van, turn to page 100.

If you decide to go right to the police, turn to page 56.

When you get to the bike shop, you find Wheels Wilson still involved with all of the riders and officials. You run into a man with a big plastic button that says OFFICIAL.

"Hi, I'm Ed Leffel. Can I help you?" he asks. Mr. Leffel tells you that he works for the Clean and Sweet Soap Company, the sponsor of the race. His job is to see that everything runs smoothly—before, during, and after the race.

When you tell him that you are covering the race for the *Dispatch,* he hands you a small folder marked PRESS KIT.

The folder is full of useful information—photos, race statistics, stories from previous races, and information about the soap company. It's just what you need for your story.

On your way back to the newspaper office, the two men you saw earlier in the day stop to talk to you. They explain that Wheels told them you were writing a story on the race.

"Come out to our van," one of them says to you. "We want to show you something for your story."

If you decide to go with them because they may have a good story, turn to page 30.

If you suspect that their story might be a hoax, turn to page 32.

122

You decide that the library might have the best information. Mr. Sam advises you to ask for Miss Swanson, the librarian.

You first call ahead, then go over to the library for a talk with Miss Swanson. She remembers that a story on the plant appeared in a national magazine about a year ago. When she gets the magazine out of the back-issue file, however, you find that the pages you need have been torn out by someone. It will take days for her to get another copy from the publisher.

You ask Miss Swanson about Cedric Wheyworth. She leads you to several magazine articles, most of which comment on his eccentric behavior. The only photograph of him that you find dates from more than twenty years ago.

In the photo, Cedric Wheyworth has dark hair and a mustache. From the articles, you find that he was a Marine in World War II. After the war, Wheyworth worked on a top-secret government project in electro-magnetics.

You ask Miss Swanson for more information about Allworth Industries, but there is nothing else available.

If you decide to go out to the plant and check out what the view of the race will look like from there, turn to page 93.

If you decide to stay at the library and do some research on the Slick Messenger Service team, turn to page 21.